Going Down Home with Daddy

For Mur and Pa, Grandma and Granddad. Thank you for the legacy and inspiration.

—K. S. L.

This book is dedicated to Azari Ayindé.

—D. M.

Author Acknowledgments

This book would not have been possible without the love and support of my family
and friends. Special thank-yous to my husband and children, illustrator Daniel Minter,
editor Kathy Landwehr and the entire Peachtree family, agent Caryn Wiseman, and
Olugbemisola Rhuday-Perkovich, Traci Sorell, Gwendolyn Hooks, Dr. Pauletta Bracy,
Bridgette A. Lacy and Dr. Nancy Tolson.

Published by
PEACHTREE PUBLISHERS
1700 Chattahoochee Avenue
Atlanta, Georgia 30318-2112
www.peachtree-online.com

Text © 2019 by Kelly Starling Lyons
Illustrations © 2019 by Daniel Minter

Edited by Kathy Landwehr
Design and composition by Nicola Simmonds Carmack
The illustrations were created in acrylic wash.

Printed in December 2018 by Tien Wah Press, Malaysia
10 9 8 7 6 5 4 3 2 1
First Edition
ISBN 978-1-56145-938-4

Library of Congress Cataloging-in-Publication Data

Names: Lyons, Kelly Starling, author. | Minter, Daniel, illustrator.
Title: Going down home with Daddy / written by Kelly Starling Lyons ;
illustrated by Daniel Minter.
Description: Atlanta : Peachtree Publishers, [2019] | Summary: Alan looks forward to the
annual family reunion at the farm where Daddy grew up, but everyone is supposed to share
something special and Alan worries about arriving with empty hands.
Identifiers: LCCN 2018008313 | ISBN 9781561459384
Subjects: | CYAC: Family reunions—Fiction. | Family life—Fiction.
Classification: LCC PZ7.L995545 Goi 2019 | DDC [E]—dc23 LC record available
at *https://lccn.loc.gov/2018008313*

Going Down Home with Daddy

Written by **Kelly Starling Lyons**

Illustrated by **Daniel Minter**

PEACHTREE
ATLANTA

On reunion morning, we rise before the sun. Daddy hums as he packs our car with suitcases and a cooler full of snacks. He says there's nothing like going down home.

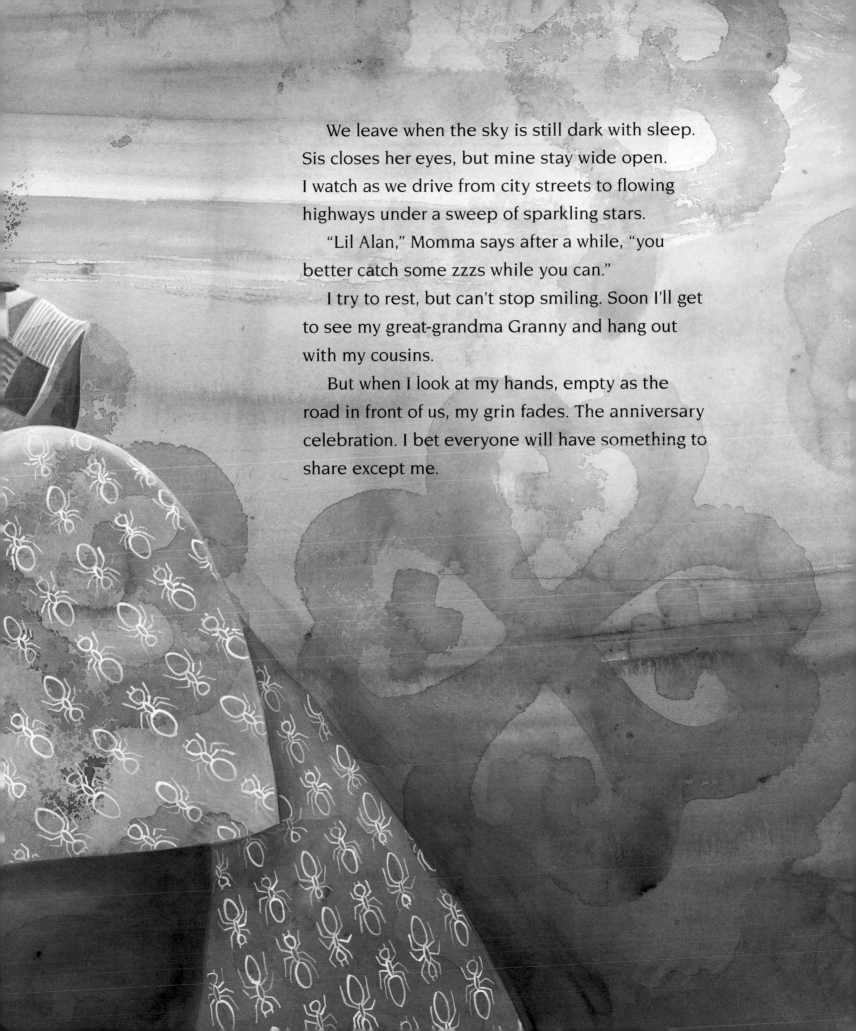

We leave when the sky is still dark with sleep.
Sis closes her eyes, but mine stay wide open.
I watch as we drive from city streets to flowing
highways under a sweep of sparkling stars.

"Lil Alan," Momma says after a while, "you
better catch some zzzs while you can."

I try to rest, but can't stop smiling. Soon I'll get
to see my great-grandma Granny and hang out
with my cousins.

But when I look at my hands, empty as the
road in front of us, my grin fades. The anniversary
celebration. I bet everyone will have something to
share except me.

I doze off in a cloud of worry and wake to sunbeams tickling my face. I squint and see a familiar John Deere tractor store and a gray silo standing at attention. We're almost there.

Sis and I sit up straight as pines when we see Granny's wood-frame house. She's right where we left her after last year's reunion, scattering corn for her chickens like tiny bits of gold.

"There she is!" Sis shouts.

Granny spreads her
arms wide and wraps us
both inside. "My, my,"
she says, and showers our
cheeks with peppermint
kisses. "I missed you so."

All afternoon, a parade of family comes home—Grandma Loretta and Grandpa James, aunts and uncles. And more cousins than I can count.

"Got a head just like your daddy," Uncle Jay teases me.

Daddy's eyes twinkle. "Now I know you're not talking about heads."

"Can't take them anywhere," Grandma Loretta says, laughing.

While the grown-ups catch up, we cousins run to the fence
to visit Granny's cows and goats.

"You doing something for the celebration?" Isaiah asks Sis.

"Singing Granny's favorite song, 'His Eye Is on the Sparrow',"
she says. "How about you?"

"Reading "Mother to Son" by Langston Hughes."

"I made a scrapbook in Granny's favorite color blue," Devin
says. "You got something, Lil Alan?"

I kick a stone and my eyes start to burn.

"Ready for a tractor ride?" Sis asks, saving me from having
to answer.

I swallow hard and climb into the trailer with Sis and Momma. I lean against the hay as Daddy drives us past the smokehouse and fishing pond and rumbles by a field dotted with puffs of white.

"Cotton has been on this land a long time, just like us," Daddy says. "Pa would drive your Uncle Jay and me on a tractor just like this one. *Look to your left*, Pa would say. *Look to your right*. The land just seemed to go on forever. *Everything you see*, Pa told us, *is ours*."

I think about what Daddy said and sit up tall. Pa is gone, but this is our time to come together and remember.

Daddy's words make me want to share more
than ever. When the ride stops, I ask him what to do.

"Think with your heart, Lil Alan," Daddy says, "that's
what Pa always told me."

Just then, we hear Granny. "Come on and get this
food while it's hot," she calls from the porch.

We dash inside. The dining room overflows with love-made dishes—smoked turkey, collards, mac and cheese, okra and tomatoes, and biscuits oozing with mayhaw jelly, just the way Daddy likes.

Hand in hand, we create a ring inside the house Pa built for Granny.

Heart to heart, we share what we're thankful for.

"Nothing is more important than family," Granny says, tearing up as she looks at every face.

Amens all around

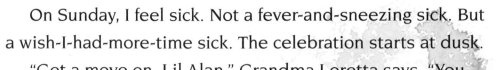

On Sunday, I feel sick. Not a fever-and-sneezing sick. But a wish-I-had-more-time sick. The celebration starts at dusk.

"Get a move on, Lil Alan," Grandma Loretta says. "You know Granny doesn't play. Growing up, we never missed a service."

At church, Daddy points to the spot where he and Uncle Jay performed a duet on trombone and trumpet.

"My hands were shaking so much I could barely play," Daddy says. "But then I saw Granny smiling. My jitters went away."

I wonder if looking at Granny will help me. But when our eyes meet, all I can think about is being the only kid with nothing to say.

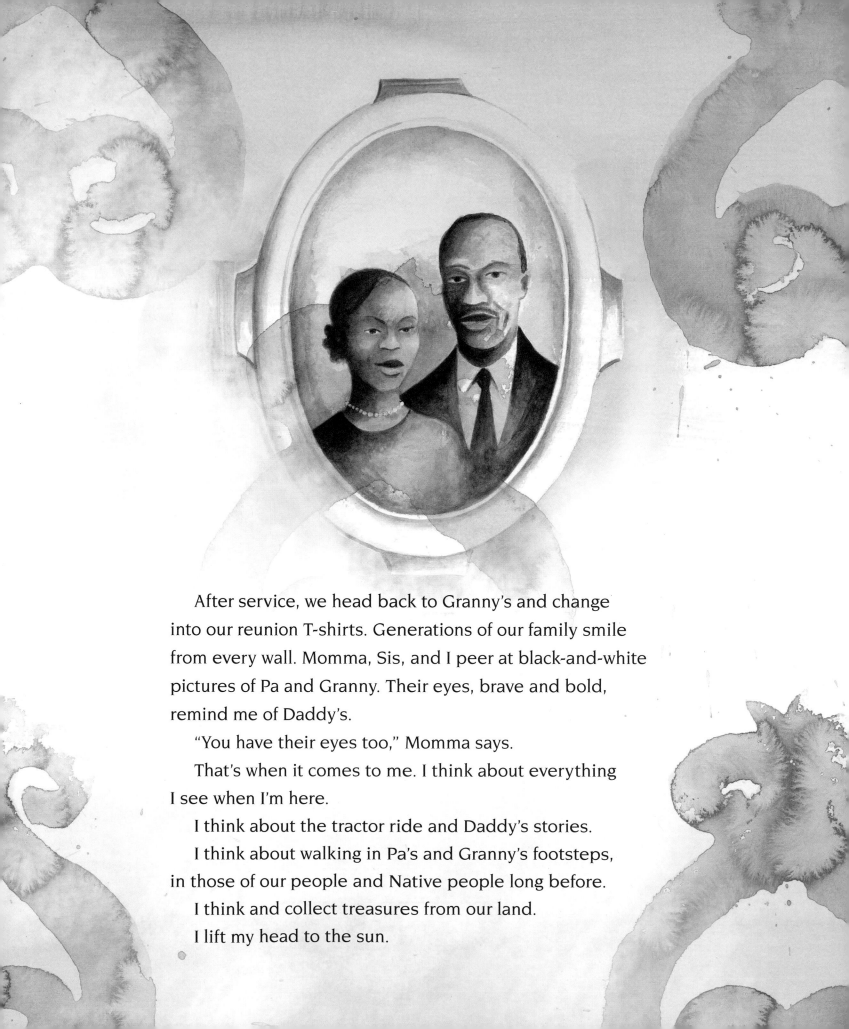

After service, we head back to Granny's and change
into our reunion T-shirts. Generations of our family smile
from every wall. Momma, Sis, and I peer at black-and-white
pictures of Pa and Granny. Their eyes, brave and bold,
remind me of Daddy's.

"You have their eyes too," Momma says.

That's when it comes to me. I think about everything
I see when I'm here.

I think about the tractor ride and Daddy's stories.

I think about walking in Pa's and Granny's footsteps,
in those of our people and Native people long before.

I think and collect treasures from our land.

I lift my head to the sun.

Just before satin night falls, we sit outside on porch steps and metal lawn chairs. It's celebration time.

"Our people were stolen from Africa and shipped to this continent in chains," Daddy says. "But no one could lock away their dreams. They dreamed on this land during slavery. They dreamed on this land as they made a way out of no way and fought Jim Crow. Seventy-five years ago, a farmer and a teacher bought this land." Daddy gazes at Granny. "And look at us now."

One after another, cousins offer their tributes. Sis's song makes Granny's eyes shine.

Isaiah's poem gets everyone nodding.

Then, I step forward.

I feel like a spotlight is blazing just on me.
I look down and say nothing.
"It's okay, Lil Alan," Sis whispers.
I lift my head and see gleaming smiles.
I try again.

"Cotton for the quilts Granny made to keep her children warm," I say, holding a white cloud in my fingers.

"A pecan for the trees Pa planted and all of the kids love to climb."

I pinch dirt and let it rain to the ground. "And earth for land that's ours as far as we can see."

Fireflies wink and whirl in a carnival around us.

"That's alright," I hear Granny say.

Daddy flashes a thumbs-up.

I grin up at the moon. It glows back at me.

"We're a mighty family!" Daddy booms.

"Mighty!" we roar back.

Then we try to make the night stretch
on forever. As grown-ups slap cards and
checkers against tables, we cousins dig
through old trunks and laugh until our hearts
explode with joy.

Too soon our goodbye morning comes.
We hug all the way to the door.
Then we climb into our car and watch
Granny and her house shrink and disappear.

When we go down home with Daddy, everything we see holds a piece of him and us. We head up the highway thinking about family and dreaming about next year.